This book has been presented to:

_____

And was first read to them by:

_____

The Reading Pig
Goes To the Library

Author—Kandy Clinkingbeard
with Nicholas I. Clement, Ed. D.

Illustrator—Judy Nostrant

The Reading Pig Goes To School. Copyright ©2018 by Nicholas I. Clement Ed. D.
Teachers Change Brains Media. All rights reserved.
Printed in the Unites States of America. No part of this book shall be used or reproduced in any manner whatsoever without written permission except in the case of brief quotations embodied in critical articles and reviews.

Teachers Change Brains Media books may be purchased for educational, business or sales promotional use.
For information – www.thereadingpig.com
Library of Congress Cataloging in Publication Data is available on request.

ISBN – 9780996389143 First edition. February 2018

Book management & marketing services – www.maxfemurmedia.com

Illustrations – Judy Nostrant

Cover layout & pre-press production — Pattie Copenhaver

Acknowledgements -

On the prompt of a colleague some years ago, I wrote a children's story. **The Reading Pig Goes To School** was the amazing result. That book project brought together a great group of people who played a variety of roles in its' success. That effort then led to this adventure, The Reading Pig Goes To The Library.

For this adventure, I have turned over the writing responsibility to Kandy Clinkingbeard – Librarian, Richardson Elementary. Kandy was an enthusiastic help with the first book and became an obvious choice to tell a tale of the pig visiting a library.

The Reading Pig project continues to thrive based on the collective and creative effort from our production team.

Judy Nostrant – Illustrator, Judy continues to amaze and delight with her work.

Pattie Copenhaver – Graphic Designer, Pattie's delicate touch brings the whole book together.

Tim Derrig – Book Manager, Tim's passion for this project from the onset is exemplary.

Rounding out the overall effort we continue to enjoy support from our friends at Pima Federal Credit Union & Simply Bits. They were among the early adopters and remain involved.
www.thereadingpig.com

My gratitude to all of you in your support of Children's Literacy.
Nic aka "Dr. C"

*Patricia Lindskog,
your love of reading
lives on.*

© 2018   Nicholas I. Clement
ISBN: 9780996389143
Published by:
Teachers Change Brains Media

www.legendaryteacher.com

The Reading Pig Goes to the Library

Foreword

Reading is a lifelong skill. No matter who we are and what we do, we will always have occasion to read daily. Whether it be from a book or a newspaper or now in the modern day, a tablet or a phone, we ALL read.

Along the way, our desire and need to read more, and more frequently, will increase based on school and career. All Children should enjoy reading. We can and should play a role in developing their love of reading. Their all-important comprehension of what they read is critical which in turn helps them succeed in life.

The Reading Pig children's book series has a two-fold purpose. First: to entertain. Second: to anchor our Children to the idea that reading is important as they develop. Whoever you are, play your part. Teach a child to read. Read to a Child. Impress upon our Children that reading is a lifelong skill.

Denise Lindskog Derrig, MA
Reading Specialist
Richardson Elementary

Enjoy the tale...

Hi, my name is Cole.
I want to tell you
about my
school library.

The kids in my class love our library day! We can learn so many ways there.

There are computers, shelves of books in neat, colorful rows and posters on the walls, but most of all, there is our Librarian!

Mrs. C
is the best!
I think
she's
part
Librarian...

...part History Teacher and part Mad Scientist!

When we go to the library we bring the reading pig. We use the reading pig when we are in a reading circle. The reading pig is squishy and has a funny nose. We pass him to each other every time the librarian turns the page.

The reading pig
makes us feel
comfortable.

The first thing you notice in our
library is a giant, inflatable
T Rex and a brontosaurus that
seems like it is alive!

There are fossils, crystals, and even a bug collection!

I asked Mrs. C if I could have my birthday party there, and that made her smile. But the best part is a humongous cage that holds a real, live snake! It makes me **shiver!**

The day Mrs. C taught us a snake lesson was the best day ever! We learned that some snakes have venom, but most snakes do not. Mrs. C read us a book about snakes. She said the book was **nonfiction**, and that meant the things we read about were true!

When it was my turn to hold the reading pig, I pretended he was a **venomous** snake.

I tried to make him bite Marcie Allen. She was annoyed. Mrs. C made me pass the reading pig to Marcie. I think Mrs. C was **annoyed** too.

When we finished the book, Mrs. C had a surprise for us. She took the snake out of his cage! Marci Allen screamed out loud, which is not following the rules of the library. But I wanted to scream a little, too.

We
were
scared!

Mrs. C told us the snake did not have venom. He liked to wrap himself around Mrs. C's arms. Once he wrapped himself around her head! We thought that was **hilarious!**

After the lesson it was time to check out books, so Mrs. C put the snake back in it's cage. All the students hurried to the nonfiction section so they could check out snake books.

I noticed that Mrs. C had not put the lock back on the snake cage. I looked at the snake's wiggling, scaly skin. I wondered what it felt like.

I was

curious.

While the rest of the class looked for books, I quietly slid open the door to the snake cage. I was sneaky. I reached in and touched the back end of the snake. It wasn't slimy! It was cool and dry!

I was **astounded**!

Mrs. C asked everyone to come check out their books. I snatched my hand out of the cage and ran over to the snake books. They were almost gone! I was sad, but Mrs. C helped me find a good one.

I felt **satisfied.**

As I took my book to the check out desk, Marcie Allen screamed loud and long! She was **terrified!**

Then I saw what Marcie saw. The snake was slithering out of the open door of his cage! All my friends must have forgotten that the snake was not venomous, because they were screaming and running for the library door. They were **frightened!** The snake was heading right toward the reading pig!

Do snakes eat pigs?
I didn't know.

I was **worried!**

I ran toward the reading
pig to rescue him from the
snake. Mrs. C told me to
stop. she said she would
get the snake. She picked
up the snake and put him
back in the cage. She wondered why the door was
open. She was **baffled**.
I was very quiet.

Mrs. C gave the signal to quiet down the class. She said the snake wouldn't hurt anyone. They felt **relieved!**

Then a funny thing happened. Mrs. C told the whole class that I was trying to protect the class from the snake. I told them I was just trying to rescue the reading pig, then they clapped for me anyway.

I felt **brave.**

When my teacher came to take us back to class, everyone told her what happened. I got to carry the reading pig back to my class. It was the best day ever!

I felt **proud!**

The End

HILARIOUS

BRAVE

Relieved

Proud *Frightened*

annoyed

comfortable

curious baffled Scared

Venemous worried

SHIVER

SATISFIED *Nonfiction*

Terrified ASTOUNDED

The Reading Pig Goes to the Library

Word Search Activity

```
I  W  W  J  Y  B  V  M  F  X  C  X  R  J  C
R  B  H  P  U  G  R  H  V  H  K  N  J  J  C
N  V  D  C  I  U  Z  A  I  E  B  D  Z  N  R
I  O  E  E  L  M  N  L  V  F  X  E  F  A  E
C  R  N  N  I  N  A  V  N  E  V  L  R  D  L
C  O  M  F  O  R  T  A  B  L  E  F  I  E  I
Z  Q  Z  Y  I  M  R  Z  I  S  V  F  G  I  E
N  R  E  O  U  C  O  O  J  W  B  A  H  F  V
T  D  U  M  P  R  T  U  W  R  R  B  T  S  E
R  S  S  Y  C  R  X  I  S  X  A  D  E  I  D
K  W  Y  D  E  D  N  U  O  T  S  A  N  T  P
B  R  G  V  O  A  O  L  R  N  E  W  E  A  R
F  N  I  S  C  A  R  E  D  H  U  A  D  S  O
R  H  T  E  R  R  I  F  I  E  D  G  W  F  U
S  U  O  I  R  U  C  Z  C  G  O  V  H  W  D
```

ANNOYED	COMFORTABLE	NONFICTION
BRAVE	HILARIOUS	SATISFIED
FRIGHTENED	RELIEVED	TERRIFIED
PROUD	SHIVER	
SCARED	WORRIED	
VENOMOUS	BAFFLED	
ASTOUNDED	CURIOUS	

CPSIA information can be obtained
at www.ICGtesting.com
Printed in the USA
LVOW05s2026190218
567069LV00001BA/1/P

9 780996 389143